WAR OF THE CHIEFTAINS

Frances Maguire

authorHOUSE®

AuthorHouse™ UK
1663 Liberty Drive
Bloomington, IN 47403 USA
www.authorhouse.co.uk
Phone: UK TFN: 0800 0148641 (Toll Free inside the UK)
      UK Local: (02) 0369 56322 (+44 20 3695 6322 from outside the UK)

Published by AuthorHouse 01/21/2022

ISBN: 978-1-6655-9611-4 (sc)
ISBN: 978-1-6655-9612-1 (hc)
ISBN: 978-1-6655-9613-8 (e)

CHAPTER 1

Please mother, please mother surely you can do something. Tell him no, begged the youngest daughter of Chieftain Alan. Stop it at once Aine, that's quite enough, her mother Agatha answered.

Look at your pale cheeks my child, have you rested at all? No, no, she wept, how could I possibly sleep knowing that my true love will die at dawn. Her mother stretches her arms towards her, she sobs on her mother's breast. True love, her mother whimpered, as she shrugged her shoulders and shook her head.

My dear child you have disobeyed your father greatly and you must be punished. You, and that boy have committed the ultimate betrayal by falling in love with one another, and not forgetting he is the son of another Chieftain. Chieftain Conall of Hendro and Bradach.

It was the Summer of 1535, when the eighteen-year-old Aine, a pretty brown eyed girl with matching brown hair, first meet her true love Fergus, a blonde, blue eyed mischievous boy. He was a helper at the 'poor house' in the village. A kind boy at heart, always keen to help others. The poor house had been established by Fergus great grandfather. It was a place the poor could come and eat. They spent whatever length of time they wanted there. Could be day's even week's especially young mothers with babies. In exchange for food and warm clothing, they looked after the land and local food stalls in the village belonging to Fergus father. Fergus loved working there. He made lots of friends and didn't mind getting stuck into whatever duties he had to do. He was a hard worker just like his father and forefathers before him. He was one of six children, three boys and three girls of Chieftain Conall and his wife Grace, supreme rulers of the provinces of Hendro and Bradach.

Although he was the second youngest son of a Chieftain and unusual for a Chieftains son to have such a common job, Fergus father let him do the things he wanted and helping the poor was very highly regarded. There was no 'airs and graces' in Conall's family, everyone was treated the same. A decent family through and through.

The same could not be said however for Aines father Alan. He was a proud and arrogant man who looked upon the lesser well of as peasants and could barely stand the sight of them.

"A waste of Space" is how he often referred to them.

She was the youngest of four children of Chieftain Alan and his wife Agatha. They reigned over the 'Mullagh' Dynasty, a much respected wealthy family from the Bradach province.

Aine was immediately attracted to the handsome carefree boy and admired his modesty and total goodness. She didn't care about who he was or where he was from, she seen no difference in anyone. You have a pure heart; she would often tell him. She found it profoundly liberating to be in the company of someone who was indeed their own person not caring what others thought.

He was so "ordinary" to be a Chieftain's son, something she could only dream of. Fergus's love for her was just the same, although he was slightly more concerned about their love for one another because of her father's nature. He knew from his own father's stories that Alan was ruthless and thought that he was, "above all others" in his eyes.

Nevertheless, their love blossomed. She would always make excuses to go the village just to meet with Fergus and sneak off to a place known as "the water's edge" just to be with him.

Not many people knew of this place. It was a beautiful quiet serene place where Fergus used to play as a child. The river flowed gently lipping around the moss-covered stones. It was surrounded by large meadows, wild trees and undergrowth and in the summer months would be an array of colour with beautiful, sweet smelling summer flowers, a truly magical place.

They would go there and laugh and play silly games together like jumping the stones to cross the river and try not to get wet.

The first one to get wet, would have to declare their love for the other. In case someone would hear them, they would say it in a language only they knew.

Their secret pact as they put it, "Ta mo chroi duitse amhain" meaning "My heart is for you only". They would fall to the ground laughing and hugging one another at this declaration.

Most of the local people from the village suspected that something untoward was going on between Fergus and Aine. Whispering amongst themselves that if her father knew it would certainly end abruptly. That wasn't on their minds as they only had eyes for each other.

Their relationship was now in its second year, and though they'd kept it secret this long that was soon coming to an end. The pair had gotten a little too carefree and naive when Fergus hadn't shown up for work at the poor house at his usual time on a bright summer morning. This was very unlike him as he was very loyal to his work.

On that mid-summer morning, it was his 20th birthday and he and Aine had arranged to meet at dawn at "the water's edge". We must meet early, he said to Aine, so I can get back to work without raising suspicion. Yes, she agreed. She had a gift for Fergus and was very excited about giving it to him. That morning she got up early around 8.00am.

She picked out a red dress one that Fergus admired before, referring to her as his "Beauty in red". She brushed her hair and washed her face and teeth. She stood in front of the mirror and told herself, today is the day I'll tell Fergus how I really feel.

Today is the day that I will tell him, I Love you. Giggling to herself she got dressed picked up her little black bag that his gift was in and left the room. Now the castle, where she lived with her family was big, and it was not going to be an easy place to leave without being seen. She and her sisters slept in the west wing of the castle. Sneaking quietly from her bedroom chamber her secret adventure was just beginning.

On the opposite side of the wide dark hallway was her sister Margaret and Roses bedroom's. The castle was very old, around six hundred years with family portraits hanging on every wall and wooden creaky floors.

She tiptoed gently trying not to place a toe on the boards that creaked, she knew exactly where they were. Stepping only on the carpet she made it to the end of the corridor without alerting her sisters or so she thought.

She didn't have to worry about her father and mother as their bedroom chamber was in the east wing of the castle. As she got to the end of the hallway she opened the large wooden door, twice her height and gently eased it closed.

She sighed as it closed for, she knew she was passed her sisters bedrooms and the rest of the way out was going to be relatively easy.

Going down the narrow stone stairs she entered the kitchen as this was easier than going past the east wing. Coming towards the Kitchen chamber she knew the head cook Imelda and her two helpers Jill and Susan would be up at their morning duties. The cooks and maids were much too busy to be interested in what the Chieftains family were up to and didn't take a second glance at Aine coming in.

She liked Imelda, she reminded her of her dear Grandmother Cassie who was now deceased. A small but broad lady, softly spoken, who was very kind and a hard worker. Morning Aine they said, morning ladies she replied as she swiftly walked on.

She wondered, what if they ask me where are I'm going? but didn't give it a second thought for now she was walking towards the back pantry on her way out. Her excitement was building as she knew she'd be meeting Fergus soon. The castle was completely surrounded by forestry.

There was a short cut to the village from the back of the castle. A narrow-wooded pathway, one she and her sister's were very familiar with. She had often used it before sneaking of to meet Fergus. Grinning broadly, feeling more confident now she was outside. She quietly stepped down onto the gravel path and starting walking as slowly as she could. Gently easing her feet down onto the noisy loose stones. Crunch, crunch she went, when suddenly a voice said.

What are you up too? Aine almost jumped out of her skin as she turned around. It was Margaret her oldest sister.

Margaret, she shrieked. What, why, are you here? Margaret, taller than her younger sister stood with her arms folded. What do you mean why am I here?

You tell me exactly what you are up to at this time of the morning? Aine was completely speechless, she was so shocked on seeing Margaret that she didn't know what to say.

She was so sure she'd gotten out without anyone seeing her. Standing there feeling embarrassed her mind was racing. Do I tell the truth and risk my father hearing this? Will I lie? she thought. Sighing heavily, she confessed and told Margaret everything. I'm meeting a boy called Fergus.

He's lovely Margaret and today is his birthday. There was no other Fergus in the village that Margaret knew of only Fergus the son of Conall. She had a sinking feeling that it was him.

7

Do you mean to tell me that you're meeting the son of Chieftain Conall? Yes, Aine reluctantly answered. What? You can't. Margaret shared the same loyal and somewhat old fashion traditional views like her father.

Although she was glad Aine told her the truth, she also knew that this "carry on" must stop and stop immediately. She was not going to let Aine betray her dear father. Are you totally out of your mind Aine? What is wrong with you? How could you do this to father? If he finds out about what you are up to his rage will not be contained. Well?

She summoned Aine back into the castle. Get back in here now she forcefully announced pointing her finger to the ground.

What, no I can't, I just can't, she answered. Margaret angrily told her, you must I tell you, you must. You listen to me young lady, your behaviour is appalling and under no circumstances can this continue. Please Margaret, just this time let me go and don't tell anyone, please for me, she anxiously begged. No, Margaret argued, it's for your own good.

At hearing this Aine was furious, for my own good. My own good is meeting with Fergus and laughing and being happy. Its miserable sitting around this lonely place following rules, being watched. Rules and traditions, I'm sick of hearing about rules and traditions. What good has that done anyone.

That's not for my own good, is it? Well Margaret, is it? I don't have to take orders from you, she boasted. Margaret's fury was growing. She caught Aine by the wrist and demanded she come back inside. Shocked at Margaret's behaviour she pulled her arm away from her.

She had never fallen out with her sister before, but she wasn't going to let anyone stop her. No one will come between Fergus and I, she proudly said and with that she ran off.

Margaret watched her as she ran away. Feeling angry she couldn't help but feel a little sorry for Aine too. The castle was a lonely place. Their father was very strict on them all and perhaps too much on Aine for she was the youngest. Feeling somewhat jealous of her sister too, for she was still to find her true love.

Although she admired her resilience, she felt humiliated at the cheekiness of Aine not listening to her. Slowly walking back inside she pondered to herself. What will I do, she thought? She knew by how Aine spoke about Fergus that it was more than a friendship. Perhaps much more. She decided to leave it for now and not speak to anyone about their argument.

CHAPTER 2

It was nearing 10 o'clock, and Fergus had already been there from 9, the exact time they were to meet. He was pacing over the mossy stones, looking around, feeling agitated. Where in God's name is she? he muttered to himself.

She said 9??? I need to go, he thought, I can't wait any longer. I'm already late. What excuse will I come up with. Just at that there was a noise coming from the bushes. As he stood by the water's edge he watched and waited nervously, desperately hoping it would be Aine, cause if not he would have a lot of explaining to do.

Finally, a pale face peeped through the rough hedging. It was Aine, breathless. He let out a huge sigh of relief. Oh, I'm so glad to see you Fergus, she joyfully whispered as she walked towards him. I wasn't sure if you'd still be here.

Yes, Aine I'm still here, he said, as he gently folded his hands around hers. Your hands Aine, they're freezing, why are you so late? Oh, it's a long story Fergus, Margaret seen me leaving, but anyway I don't want to think of that...she paused to catch her breath…Happy Birthday Fergus, she said lovingly, gazing into his eyes.

He gently pulled her towards him and hugged her. His nose caressed her ear as he caringly whispered. Thank you my "beautiful beauty in red". Slowly emerging from their embrace, she said, Fergus there's something I want to tell you.

He stared into her beautiful brown eyes. What is it Aine he quietly asked? Fergus…I Love You. Fergus took a small step back, a warm smile broke out on his face, blushing slightly. He knew at that very moment he too was in love.

They had spent so many happy days together at this beauty spot but today seemed different. It felt magical. It was as if their souls had come together as one.

As the sun began to peak through the cloudy sky, its rays shone brightly on the spot where they stood. Aine, I love you too. Holding her hands, he slowly began to move towards her.

She stood quietly with bated breath. He leaned in and gently kissed her soft warm lips. Their first kiss. As he did, he wrapped his arms around her small frame, holding her tightly, she embraced him too.

The joy they felt at that precious moment would always remain in their hearts. A moment neither one would ever forget or more importantly would never want to forget. Gently easing his lips from hers he whispered, "Ta mo chroi duitse amhain". (My heart is for you only). Aine was overjoyed.

The panic she had encountered earlier with her sister was a distance memory now. In a dreamy state of mind, she didn't care if Margaret was going to tell or not. Fergus's love for her was more important and powerful than anything. Feeling so in love, she almost forgot about the present she'd brought for him. Oh, Fergus I almost forgot, I have brought you a special gift for your birthday.

She reached into her black bag still strapped across her chest and took out a little white box. Here this is for you. Ah, Aine really? There was no need to get me anything, he explained. I wanted to get you something special, and I do hope you like it.

He slowly opened it and inside was a silver coin, a coin he gave her when they first met. On one side it had his families Coat of Arms with Fergus name inscribed underneath. Aine had kept it all this time and had her Coat of Arms inscribed on the other side also bearing her name.

Oh, my dear Aine, you still have it? he laughed. Yes, she giggled. It's got both our names on it now and that way when we're apart you only have look at it to think of me. Fergus, gently touching her cheek moved her hair behind her ear and told her. I don't need anything to remind me of your beautiful face.

I just close my eyes and your there... Thank you my darling. I'll cherish it fondly as he put it into his waistcoat pocket.

It was 10.30 now and Fergus knew he had to get to work. My dear Aine I need to go, although our meeting was brief, he explained, it was wonderful.

Yes, she answered truly wonderful. I'll go now and God willing I'll see you soon. Oh yes, she confidently said, tomorrow? I hope to see you tomorrow. kissing her cheek, he reluctantly left going through "Rhododendron Lane", a flowering pink hedgerow that led to the high street side of the village.

Aine watched as he disappeared from her sight. She sat down on a stone, smiling from ear to ear. I'm so happy she told herself, so happy. Gazing into the water she started to worry about what happened earlier with Margaret.

I wonder did she tell Rose or mother or worse, father, did she tell my secret? With that worrying thought she got up and left.

Now this behaviour was totally unforgiving within the protocol of the House of Mullagh where Aines father reigned. Furthermore, Chieftain Alan, Aines father, despised Chieftain Conall. He was wealthier and much more popular with helping the poor and downtrodden. Forty years earlier his father John defeated Alan's father Patrick in what became known as the great battle of "Morris Hill". After long years of fighting and bloodshed between the families, it was agreed by both clans that battle was the only way to settle their differences once and for all. And so it was, they prepared their loyal men for battle. There was only going to be one Supreme leader when all was over.

Several hundred good men lost their lives on Morris Hill on that Easter Monday morning. It was a terrible and bloody battle that lasted three long days. On losing the battle Patrick lost his power to rule over the southern province of Bradach.

This province had been under the control of Alan's family for generations making them ruler over half the lands of ancient Ireland. But the loss meant that Alan was now under the rule of Conall. To add more insult to their already tarnished defeat, not only was he the new Chieftain of The Province of Bradach, but Conall's family were already Chieftains of the Hendro province and was now known as a Supreme High Chieftain. The highest honour in all the lands. The bitterness and defeat remained very deep and was very vivid in Alan's memory. He was 19 years old when this great battle took place. His father whom he adored died shortly afterwards. He vowed on his father's deathbed that he would reign once more, but that day had yet to come.

Following his defeat, access to profitable trading of spices, cloves, silks and jewels had all but gone leaving him less well off. He wasn't one for following rules either or taking any orders from anyone and in Conall's goodness he didn't enforce his law upon Alan. Rather he was just content to keep away from him altogether. Even though he was now a

Supreme High Chieftain, Conall respected that Alan was still a Chieftain.

This was still a position of great strength. Coming from the house of Mullagh, a well-respected Dynasty for hundreds of years, Alan still had his title and with it still ruler over certain things. For instance, twenty percent of the village people where his workers. His beloved castle sat on two thousand acres of land. He still had a huge following of men known as his loyal Clansmen who would lay down their life for him and his family.

CHAPTER 3

It wasn't long until the castle came into view. Aine's heart began to beat faster. Right, she said perking her shoulders back and head up.

I will just have to face whatever is to come. Slowly walking back inside she took the side door through the study. This door would have been locked earlier. She briskly walked on through the study, continuing into the library. It felt like all the eyes of the portraits hanging on the dark red walls were watching her every move. Finally, she came out into the west wing and back upstairs to her bedroom.

She entered the room and quietly closed the door behind her. Well, she proudly said to herself that wasn't as bad I thought it would be.

She started getting undressed. Reaching into the wardrobe for the clothes hanger she could still smell Fergus cologne. Taking a deep breath, the loved-up Aine fell onto the bed. Suddenly Knock, Knock, Aine sprung up as fast as she could and in a shaky voice answered yes, who is it?

It's your mother. Can I come in. Of course, mother. Opening the door slowly she came in. Morning Aine. Morning mother, she replied, waiting on her mother to ask what had she been up too? Her mother looked around the room and walked towards the window silently.

The silence was deafening, it seemed to last for ages for Aine. You could have heard a pin drop. So, you had a sleep-in today Aine? Ahh had I or I mean yes mother I did have a sleep in, she slowly answered. Her mother turned towards her. Aine was now feeling more and more anxious waiting on her mother to say something. I wondered why you would be having a sleep in on such an important day, explained her mother.

Important day? Aine replied with a confused look on her face. Yes, my dear child, have you forgotten. Well kind of. Honestly Aine you have a head on you like a sieve. Today is the day for your fathers annual "Knightly sports". Oh yes mother that, no I did remember, but you know I just thought it would be later in the afternoon that's all. Her mother wasn't very convinced by Aine's story. Very well my dear, get yourself organised and meet with us all in the Grand Hall at noon.

Oh my, Aine thought to herself, how did I possibly forget about today. Perhaps it's because I'm in love, she thought laughing to herself.

The Knightly Sports was the biggest day of Chieftain Alan's annual events. There were several small events through the year, but none compared to this one. He would put on a show like no other. This day was above all others. His day to dress in his finest attire. His day to show off his family. He wanted the local people to see the grandeur of his castle. To show off and let everyone know that he was richer than them. The dress code was bright rich colours of silk or satin and shiny jewels. He would have his footman buy in the finest cuts of meat.

His maids would have sourced the finest whiskeys, wines and spirits. These drinks would only be given to the Knights and noblemen. The beer was for the peasant people. Although Alan had no great desire to have these kinds of people at the castle, his wife encouraged him to do so as it was the right thing to do, she told him. After all they work for you in the village, making us money on their stalls. Reluctantly, he would give into her reminding his wife that under no circumstances where they allowed in to the castle. Only in the forecourt and surrounding areas. Nevertheless, this was always a day of great fun and laughter.

Margaret had been with her sister Rose in the study for most of the morning after her confrontation with Aine. They were beautifully dressed for the big occasion. What do you think I should do Rose? Margaret asked. Rose was very close to her younger sister.

They both had their mother's nature, loving and kind-hearted. Margaret certainly was her father's daughter. A no nonsense person. I do feel very angry at Aine for being this silly at believing this alliance of hers is something she sees as desirable, she tuttered.

Rose was also shocked and disappointed. They, as her older sisters always guided her and were always encouraged by their parents to teach her good standards and instil in her loyalty for a girl in her position. You know Margaret, Rose explained, if you confide in mother about this the blame may well be on us too. This was something Margaret contemplated. Let's just wait and see. We shall take her aside today and perhaps after your argument earlier she will have explained to him that they cannot meet anymore, Rose encouraged.

Oh, I don't think so Rose. You should have seen her, all dressed up and so adamant to be with him. I do worry for her. If father finds out about this, God above only knows what will happen, sighs Margaret. Well let's put this behind us for now it's almost noon and we have a big day ahead, Rose said as she walked out.

They made their way to the grand hall, and upon their entrance Aine was already there with her parents.

Margaret would not make eye contact with her. Aine had guessed that she hadn't said to anyone about earlier. By now the crowds were gathering outside. The noise of excitement was building. Alan donned a pale taupe satin shirt, a traditional colour his forefathers wore, tucked neatly into his black trousers matching his knee-high boots. On his shoulders was a large fox's fur cape adorned with his neckpiece made from silver and encrusted with jewels. Hanging in the centre of it he proudly wore a golden circular piece with the "Mullagh" crest on it. A show of strength and defiance.

Agatha looked radiant in a blue full length tunic gown. She wore a matching cape and smaller jewels around her neck.

Aine wore an emerald-green gown, with her hair tied back with jewels. She thought perhaps Fergus might chance making his way in today as the grounds where open to everyone. But then again after all that happened, he probably wouldn't. The family were now ready standing proudly, Alan turned to his doormen and instructed them to open the doors.

There the family were greeted with cheers from the large crowd. They slowly walked out; Alan lifted his arm to salute the people.

In a loud voice he said. I, the great Chieftain Alan of Mullagh declare the games to begin, and with that they cheered, and the fun began. The family made their way through the crowds to view what was on show.

There were stalls of food and drink for people to partake in Alan's good cheer. The Knights took part in mock battles called tournaments. Two knights would go face to face in a jousting competition.

The winners of the tournaments would win valuable prizes and more importantly the admiration of the young noblewomen who were in attendance.

There were birds of prey showing of their skills hunting other birds. Margaret made sure that she would keep as far away as possible from Aine.

She didn't want anything to ruin her father's day. Meanwhile Aine was feeling relaxed as she already had guessed her parents hadn't heard or things would have been very different.

Aine had met with her friend Tara, a local girl who worked with Fergus. Honestly Tara I couldn't believe my eyes when I seen Margaret at the door, she laughed. What about Fergus, did he get into trouble when he arrived late at work? Not really, Tara explained. You know Fergus everyone loves him at work, and no one really questioned why he was late. They must have just thought he slept in. Oh, and Aine he told me to let you know that he better not show up today after what happened. Yes Tara, he's right. As much as I'd love to see him, I don't want any more arguments today.

The day wore on and it was now time for the traditional evening ball in the Grand Hall. Only the knights and their families and other people of importance were given permission from Alan to enter.

Aine feeling tired went to her bedroom. Passing Roses bedroom, she thought to herself. Wonder is Rose there? Knowing that she would be much more sympathetic to her than Margaret, she quietly knocked. Rose are you in there?

Yes, I am Rose answered. May I come in please. You may. Aine nervously opened the door, keeping her head bowed as she entered.

Sit over here Aine beside me. She walked over, sat down beside Rose at her dressing table. Rose turned towards her. Aine's hands were fidgeting. So Rose, were you talking to Margaret?

Yes of course I was Aine, you hardly think that Margaret could keep that to herself. Oh, I know. It's just that I really like him.

Rose perking up her shoulders explained. Look at me Aine, this is a very serious situation. I'm not sure you know just how serious it is. This is above all the worst betrayal on the family. Did you not listen to anything I taught you growing up?

Aine was feeling so bad for Rose. She loved her sister dearly, but Rose what I can I do? I do really love him. I think about him all the time. I dream of being with him. He loves me too. I cannot help how I feel towards him Rose, said Aine as she started to cry.

I'm not giving up on him, I just won't. I'm willing to risk what is to come.

On hearing this Rose had the same sinking feeling Margaret had. She knew that trying to persuade her to change her mind wasn't going to happen. She could see the deep love she had for him in her eyes. Oh Lord help us; I don't know what to say, she sighed.

Pausing for a minute she looked at Aine and whispered. I can't believe what I'm going to say to you but, swallowing deeply she said in a firm voice. You'll have to leave or run away. I don't know what else to say.

If father hears of this either you or Fergus will be taken to the "Black Park".

And you know what will happen. Aine's face went as white as a ghost. Nodding her head slowly, she knew that meant one thing and one thing only. DEATH, death by hanging. The "Black Park was a horrible ruthless place with a dark past of torture and humiliation that ended in death.

The Gallows stood tall in this lonesome place surrounded by tall dark trees. It had an eerie presence. There was a ghostly feeling of the poor souls that had lost their lives here were still roaming around.

Named the "black park" for its gruesome act, people were publicly hung for all to see.

This ultimate humiliation was to be a reminder that no one would disobey their ruler. Not even family.

The two sisters sat there in silence. Rose hugged her as the tears welled up in her eyes, she encouragingly said.

I'll help you Aine, I'll help you escape. It's the only thing you can do. With her head bowed, Aine asked her. What about Margaret? What about mother? Leave it to me, Rose answered. But don't tell anyone about what we discussed. First, we must come up with a plan.

CHAPTER 4

Alan and Agatha were seated before a table laden with a plethora of scrumptious food. The ball had been underway now for some time.

People were enjoying good food and wine, and many were dancing. Alan leaning sideways to Agatha asked. Where are our daughters? They should be here, dancing with these fine wealthy men that would make a suitable husband. Yes, she wondered. Oh, I'm sure they're around here somewhere. It's so crowded perhaps they're dancing already.

She called her aide Jane over to find the girl's. Let them know Jane that the ball will soon be over, and they need to be here for the final dance. Yes, my lady, and of Jane went.

Margaret was still out in the forecourts enjoying the company of the handsome Knights. She felt that she had to tell on Aine and by doing so would get full admiration from her father. Something she always yearned for.

She hadn't seen the girls for a while now and wondered about this believing Rose had probably took Aine to one side to tell her off. Enjoying the company of the men too much she decided to not say anything until the following day. After all she didn't want to ruin her father's big event.

Meanwhile, Aine and Rose were busy packing a small suitcase. Where will I go Rose?

I've a good friend in the village that you can go to tonight. Tonight? said Aine; Yes tonight. You can't wait until tomorrow. Tonight, will be perfect. With all that's going on, no one will notice us leaving. We can sneak away quietly, and I will just pretend to know nothing. Oh yes Rose good thinking. But remember Aine we must go down for the last dance. You know father's knightly tradition. He wants to be the one to find us a "husband". Rolling her eyes at Rose, Aine agreed.

Of course, God forbid if we picked one ourselves.

I'll go with you when all is over, but we must pick our time as to be careful not to get caught. Alright answered Aine. Putting her hand on Rose's shoulder she said, thank you so much Rose for understanding. It means so much to me to have your assurance and support. I will be forever in debt to you. Rose smiled at her, come on let's just get you there safely first.

They decided that the after midnight would be best. Hopefully by that time everyone will have gone to bed.

Margaret and father will have taken enough wine to keep them sleeping till morning. Yes, agreed Aine. Rose left the room to go back to the dance. Don't be too long Aine, she said leaving. She sat on the bed, feeling worried with a tinge of anticipation.

I'll write a note for Fergus she thought, to explain what's going on and Rose will see that he gets it for me.

So, she started...Dearest Fergus,

I'm writing to you with great love and affection.

Remember earlier I told you Margaret seen me leaving to meet with you.

I fear my father might hear of this, so I, with the help of my dear sister Rose will leave the castle tonight at midnight.

I hope to see you very soon, then we can be together forever.

Yours lovingly Aine.

She tucked the note inside the suitcase and left the room.

Rose was explaining to her mother that she and Aine had been in the study and that Aine would be down soon. Her mother thought little of it and continued enjoying the evening.

Shortly afterwards Aine joined them. Jane was only now making her way to the west wing to find the girls for their mother.

She got held up helping the kitchen staff chase out one of the birds from the games that escaped into the kitchen.

She walked to Rose's room, knocked, waited but got no reply. She then tried Aine's bedroom. Hello, she said knocking firmly. Is anyone in? Nothing, not a sound. She thought she'd best enter the room as Agatha would want an answer to the whereabouts of the girls.

Opening the door, she peeped in. No one was there. That's strange she thought, they're not downstairs either. Being nosey Jane couldn't help herself but walk on in. They were never allowed into the girl's rooms without permission.

She quietly entered the room. Looking around to see what she could see. She started rummaging through Aine's personal thing's when she noticed the suitcase.

Wait, she thought, a suitcase on the bed? That's odd. With a puzzled look on her face, she slowly walked over. Opening the case, she was shocked to see it was packed full. She hurried back to the door gently closing it. I'll have a peek inside she thought.

As she was in Aine's bedroom she knew it had to be her suitcase. But why? she wondered. Why would she have a suitcase packed? Where is she going? Rooting through her clothes, there was the note with Fergus name on it. Her eyes lit up, opening it she began to read. Oh my, she said to herself, Aine's in love and going to run away. She could barely believe what she was reading. She sat down on the bed. I must tell Agatha, I must. I must tell before she leaves. She folded the Letter and pushed it into her pocket, then quietly left the room.

Little did the sisters know what was going on. Jane hurried along the large hallway making her way downstairs into the grand Hall. Rose and Aine were now dancing with their "chosen" husband for the last dance.

In a blind panic Jane couldn't find Agatha. She didn't see her in the Hall. On her way outside she bumped into Margaret who was making her way inside. Slow down Jane, you almost tossed me over. Is there something wrong? No, no it's nothing. I'm fine.

You don't look fine to me, you look very flustered, are you alright? No honestly, I'm fine, thank you.

She walked away but Margaret knew something wasn't quite right.

She followed her without her knowing and it wasn't long until she'd found Agatha.

Excuse me my lady, she gracefully said, can I have a quiet word with you. Oh no not now Jane. It's the final dance and I'm looking for Margaret. Oh, there you are Margaret. Come, hurry, father has a lovely young man for you to dance with. Turning to Jane she explained, wait at my chambers until the dance is over and you can have a word with me then. Yes, my lady. Off they went leaving Jane standing there. The last dance was in full swing. Agatha, always the pleasing wife and hoping one of her daughters would find a nice man to settle down with was eager to please Alan. The last dance of the night was special to her as this was how she met and fell in love with him.

A romantic waltz could be heard playing throughout the castle. Every year was the same. Alan would hand pick certain men for his girls. They had to be of a particular standard. RICH!!! Holding the girls tightly, the men would glide and sway them round the floor looking more for Alan's approval than theirs. This was not at all pleasing to the girls and luckily it didn't last long for now the dance was over and once again no suitable matches this year either. Aine didn't care, she already had her match, albeit under strained circumstances. They kindly thanked the gentlemen for the pleasure and much to their disappointment none of them were suitable. Margaret scurried of the dance floor to her mother. Jane needs you, she said. She wanted to tell you something. Remember? Yes, alright Margaret, what's the panic? I'll go now. Margaret went with her mother.

Agatha left and made her way to meet Jane. Jane, she said as she approached her. Why were you in such a hurry to talk to me? What was so important?

I'm really sorry Agatha but when you asked me to look for the girls, I came across this letter in Aine's room. A letter? Come in here and sit-down Jane. You wait outside Margaret.

Taking the letter out of Jane's hand she read it slowly and loudly. Agatha fell back into her chair. Her face drained of its colour. What on earth? Where was this? And who on earth is Fergus? she said, raising her voice.

It was in a suitcase packed full on her bed. SUITCASE???? Packed full on her bed? she said as she raised her voice even louder. I'm really sorry my lady to tell you about this awful news on such an occasion but I just had to.

No, No, Agatha explained, you were indeed very right to tell me. Alan will be outraged.

With that Margaret walked in. I knew this mother from this morning, I warned her about this terrible situation, but she wouldn't listen. I couldn't tell you or father until tomorrow, I couldn't possibly disappoint my dear father on his big day. Agatha shook her head in disbelief. Does Rose know about this too she asked. Yes, answered Margaret. I told her about our argument this morning. Staring at Margaret, Agatha asked. Who is Fergus? Well mother that's the biggest problem of all. He is, em, he is.... WHO Margaret? spit it out. He's Chieftain Conall's son. There I said it. WHAT!!!! Agatha sat motionless, shaking her head. I can't believe it.

How could she? What must she be thinking? Did you know that she was planning on running away Margaret? No mother I had no idea that she was planning this.

Right, Agatha said as she stood up. Jane not a word of this can be mentioned to anyone, do you understand?

Yes, my lady you have my word, and she left the room. Now mother, you must tell father.

Margaret this is not your concern now, it is mine to deal with. But mother! Margaret, I said this is none of your concern, I will deal with this in my own good time. Agatha was inwardly concerned. She knew someone was going to pay a high price but also knew this had to come to an end. Margaret, she said, will you please leave my room I want to be left alone. Yes, mother.

Margaret's anger was growing. It was as if no one was taking this seriously.

CHAPTER 5

Rose and Aine were feeling a little more relaxed now, hoping that their idea for later would all go to plan. It was approaching 10 o'clock and the evening's entertainment was coming to an end.

Agatha had composed herself for now and joined her husband again before the grand finally. It was now the end of the great "knightly sports".

Alan stood up and declared the night a great success and now over. A little worse for wear he thanked his loyal people for their loyalty and left to go to his chamber.

Agatha accompanied him out. Through the rush of people leaving, Margaret made her way over to Aine and Rose. Mother knows, she told them with joy in her voice. She knows and she will tell father, or I will.

Margaret not forgetting how angry she felt earlier when Aine wouldn't listen to her now had her chance to get her own back. What? No Margaret, please say it's not so. It is so Aine. Filled with fear she ran off to hide. Rose confronted Margaret. Why did you tell her, you know what might happen? I didn't tell Rose dear, it was Jane, mothers' aide. She went looking for you two earlier and found some stupid letter of Aine's in her room. What on earth are you thinking, helping her to escape?

Oh no, I don't believe it? Rose muttered quietly. And anyway Rose, why are you defending such appalling behaviour?

Catching Margaret's arm, she pulled her aside. Listen Margaret, she will not see another birthday if father hears this.

Father will condemn them both to death. Look what happened to Darragh our dear brother. He only escaped death because Malda was killed instead. I can't bear to think of losing another family member.

Well, she should have thought about that before meeting with that boy.

He's a man and she's a woman, Rose said angrily. Margaret shrugged herself away from Rose. You would actually take her side over father. You too would risk the fall of our Dynasty Rose. You're as bad as her.

Well, I'm not like you. I will defend my father and this house of Mullagh till the day I die, and no one Rose, no one will change or destroy that. This is not about sides Margaret. This is about life and death. It's that serious!! Well then Rose, you've made your mind up on where your loyalty lies, and I know where mine lie. Margaret turned away and sharply walked down the corridor and out of Rose's sight. Rose stood there bewildered.

She thought quickly. Right, I need to get Aine out of here now and fast. She run as fast as she could to their bedroom chamber.

Aine was quite aware that her father would be in a blistering rage, she had seen it all too many times before after he had his son Darragh, her beloved brother whom she was very fond of sent away to Crilly, a place no one wanted to go for his drunkenness and foolery with his second Cousin Malda.

Crilly was a place of hard labour and torture prison-like, ruled by the Mullagh Dynasty. Alan had no mercy whatsoever on Darragh and made sure he was worked more than the others.

Darragh was a bright boy but like his own father adored women and felt he could have anyone he could.

But his father Alan was jealous of his only son for he had taken his father's mistress Malda from him.

Alan adored Malda and had been having a secret affair for years. Agatha knew all about it, but it was much easier to turn a blind eye and keep the peace. However, Malda was a flirtatious woman and soon had her eye fixed on the handsome young son instead. It wasn't long until she and Darragh started their raunchy affair. It was short-lived though. Alan soon heard of it and was outraged.

Malda was put to death in the `Black Park` and Darragh had to swear under an old tradition that came from "Valley of the Hawthorn tree" that he would not return until after his father's death. It was believed and revered that if you broke the "hawthorn" tradition all sorts of ghostly anguish would accompany you till your death.

On opening the large wooden door of the bedroom chamber, Rose was stopped right there where she stood still holding the door handle. She looked up and there her father stood with a look on his face that could kill with one stare.

He was a menacing figure most of the time but in his rage looked larger than is 6'5 and nineteen stone frame. The anger in his eyes was one of terror. It was quite clear that he had been told what was going on.

Agatha was with him trying to calm him down.

He was outraged, frothing as he grit his teeth at Rose. WHERE is Aine, he roared. Rose was terrified at this sight. Please father, I don't know.

Yes, you do, tell me, he shouted. Aine was in her room and could hear what was going on out in the hallway. She was so frightened, she got her suitcase of the bed and pushed it underneath to hide it. She had nowhere to go only sit and wait and hope her father would not come in.

Agatha still trying to calm Alan down but to no avail. He stormed passed Rose almost knocking her to the ground.

Where are you going, Agatha worryingly asked but got no reply. Agatha knew that he would be angry but didn't contemplate just how angry. She was beginning to regret telling him at all.

She told Rose to look for Aine and keep her out of her father's sight. Mother, why did you tell him? Rose, oh dear Rose, I don't know, I didn't realise he was going to be this angry. I was foolish to think this way. Alan went outside to the forecourt looking for his trusted aide Dalton. He was his faithful servant. He was always looking for ways to please Alan and this was going to be his perfect opportunity. He would never let him down and Alan was going to need him now more than ever.

On seeing Dalton, Alan summoned him to find "that boy" as he put it. Bring him to me, he demanded. Keep guard at Aine's bedroom and watch her every move.

Alan was even more enraged when he found out that it was Chieftain Conall's son. He seen this as a total mockery of his family. Making a fool of him.

As far as Alan was concerned, Fergus was making a fool of his daughter and that he really didn't love her or even have feelings for her.

He was just using her to get at her family. He even suggested to Agatha that Chieftain Conall probably "put the boy up to it".

He will not make a fool out of me, he demanded. Never! Never!

This was Alan's chance to get his own back on Conall. All the years of hurt, anger, resentment was now coming to the fold.

With his hand on his chest Dalton sincerely declared, I will see to it Chieftain Alan, that the boy will be seized. Dalton rounded up his most trusted clansmen to start the search for Fergus.

Rose was now with Aine. She sat sobbing heavily at her bedroom window watching what was going on outside.

Rose I'm so afraid now. If they find Fergus, father will have him killed. Poor Fergus Rose, poor Fergus, she cried loudly.

Sshh Aine ssh. You'll have to pull yourself together. We have little time now. But I can't possibly escape now Rose. Father has the castle surrounded. Yes, yes, I know, ahh this is not going to be easy I know. Look Aine, you will not be able to leave tonight, that you are right about.

Just stay here and hope that father doesn't come looking for you. He's beyond angry, so when I leave the room, lock your door and if he knocks pretend your sleeping, alright.

Nodding slowly and with a heavy heart she agreed. I will think of something, Rose encouragingly told her.

Agatha took Alan to their chambers to try to calm him down. You must rest now Alan, she told him. That's enough activity for one evening, don't you think. Alan still in a rage didn't reply. Everyone was exhausted. The day had been a great success but had now taken a turn for the worse.

CHAPTER 6

Two weeks had now passed and just when Alan had almost given up all hope of imprisoning Fergus, he was captured. He hadn't spoken to Aine in all that time. She was confined to her chambers mainly, although she occasionally went for a walk with Rose, only around the castle grounds.

Word had got to Fergus that Alan had his clansmen out hunting for him. He had managed to escape them for this long.

Then one for the villagers under threat by Dalton, told him of Fergus whereabouts. He was captured easily in the middle of the night as he slept.

It was a long two weeks for Aine. She hadn't seen Fergus in all that time. On Rose's advice she didn't make any attempt to leave the castle. This would have been much too risky.

Morning dawned on yet another lonely day. Aine jumped from her bed.

She had the same thought today as she had every day since the night of the "knightly Sports".

She sat motionless, have they found him yet? She wondered.

It wasn't long until a knock came to the door. Aine, it's me Rose. Slowly going over and opening the door, Rose came in. She had that empty look on her face. They seized him Rose didn't they, Aine bravely asked. Yes, she quietly answered.

Last night, while he slept. I knew it was going to be easy to capture him, Aine answered.

I honestly hoped after all this time that he might have gotten away. I even thought perhaps he's gone back to Hendro to be with his family.

Fergus was now a prisoner of Alan.

He told Dalton to "prepare the `Black park` for the next morning. I'm taking no chances with this one, he must be got rid of.

Fergus was taken to the prison tower within the castle grounds. Put him into the cellar of the tower, Alan told the guards. He won't be here long anyway. His fate is now in my hand's.

How dare he try to destroy my Dynasty, he shouted, as he pounded his fist on his chest.

Your forbidden to leave your room Aine now, for fear you might have Fergus released, Rose told her.

That didn't matter to her now. I don't care Rose if I'm never allowed to leave this room again. Taking her hand

Rose sat down beside her. Aine, all is not lost yet. Yes, he might be captured, but perhaps mother might change his mind. That is just ludicrous Rose, Aine said shaking her head. Not ever would father change his mind especially not for something like this.

Rose knew Aine was right. It is what it is now Rose. I can only pray something will intervene in this terrible situation.

They sat quietly.

There might be something else we can do, Rose said in a puzzling voice.

Aine looking at her with a frown, what? What exactly are you talking about?

Well, there is this kind of spell. It's very ancient. You know the old man John from the village? Yes, Aine replied with interest. My friend Sarah told me about him.

Well apparently, it comes from down the generations of his family. Old man John is "a seventh son" of "a seventh son", and it's believed that because of this he himself can do special things, sort of like, he has some kind of special powers. What kind of special things? asked Aine.

Well, Rose sighed, I don't really know but I heard of stories from the past that he can help people with all sorts of problems.

Goodness me Rose. Are you trying to tell me he can free Fergus because that would be a miracle? Rose spoke on. People that disappeared before, strangely returned after visiting John. Aine was quiet, inside a little glimmer of hope was emerging.

Look Rose I will do anything to help Fergus, but you'll have to be the one to visit John. I know. I will go to his house in the village today, said Rose. It's all we've got.

She hugged Aine and promised she'd do her very best. The rest of the family were still angry with Aine and decided to leave her on her own. Her father was just happy to have Fergus imprisoned. He would deal with Aine later. His loyal clansmen took turns guarding her room.

Rose sat of and it wasn't long till she made her way to old man John's house in the village. The house was very old and run down. She stood still looking at the house. He'll think I'm crazy, she thought.

The pathway leading up to the door was overgrown with thorny bushes and brambles.

Ducking her way through she came to the door. Knock, Knock. Nothing, not a sound. Hello, she called, hello, is there anyone there? A small window to her left opened slightly. Who goes there?

Expecting someone to open the door instead, Rose started stuttering. Oh em, my name is Rose and em, well.... em. What? Spit it out, a grumpy voice shouted.

She leaned closer to the window. Where are you? I can't see you, but I hear your rudeness, she boldly told him.

Just then the door opened. There stood a little old man all four foot of him with long grey hair.

Oh, hello. My name is Rose, she said as she looked down and stretched out her hand.

There's no need for handshakes, come in. Rose was a little weary but regardless walked on in.

He led her down a dark hallway, into the most cluttered room she'd ever been in. There were books everywhere. The floor was covered with large flagged flat stones. One of the walls was covered in clocks. They ticked and tocked loudly in rhythm with one another. There were cats of all colours roaming around giving her a look of 'why are you in my house'.

Sit down if you can find somewhere to sit, he said as he pointed to a pile of papers on a chair.

No thank you, I'm quite alright, I won't keep you too long.

He sat down on a three-legged stool by an open fire on the floor. My, you have a lot of books. Do you like reading? And you have a lot of cats. I love cats. Is your name old man John? Why all the questions? he asks, staring at Rose. I'm sorry, Rose answered.

So, what do you want from me, he questioned? Well, I don't know if you can help me or not, she explained. With a cross look on his face, he turned towards her.

I'll be the judge of that, now what do you want? Rose's patience's was wearing thin.

Look my sister's sweetheart is in great danger. My father has him imprisoned and he will die tomorrow morning. I really need your help.

Your sister's lover? Well... Why isn't she here then?

She is forbidden to leave her room. Look, Rose said in a cross voice. I've heard stories about you that you have some magical powers or something like that?

John laughed hysterically almost falling of his tiny stool. Magical powers? That's the best I've heard in a long time. Oh, oh, oh, hahaha......

Rose was not impressed and was beginning to think this was a total waste of her precious time.

Look, she shouted over his laughing. Can you help me or not you rude, silly little man?

Just with that, silence... He stood up and looked at her. Paused for a minute... Yes, I can, but you'll have to help me in order for it to work.

Alright, Rose answered. What do you need me to do?

Well, they like gift's, he whispered...They? Gifts? Rose answered. Yes, I tell you, gifts. You can't get something for nothing, he boldly told her. Nodding her head, she listened.

You must bring me a strand of your sister's hair, but only a strand from behind her ear.

48

I also need a piece of clothing belonging to her, but nothing with buttons on it.

You'll need to come with me.... you are a blood relative of her's? Yes, she answered. Good he replied. But where are we going, I thought I just had to come here.

Goodness no, no, he laughed. We must go to Hawthorn Hill. That's where they live. They live? Rose asked. Stop asking me question's, he said raising his voice.

Now bring these thing's back to me, but it must be before sunset, and I will break the "prisoners curse".

I will, I will, Rose said eagerly, thank you and I'm sorry for being cross. Please leave now, he grumpily replied.

Rose hurried back knowing she hadn't much time. She burst into Aine's room. Aine, I think it's going to work. I honestly believe this little rude man can help. Seriously Rose?

Aine was so excited. Rose you are a darling. So how can he help? Look, pull a hair from behind your ear and give it to me. What? Really? Aine asked.

Yes, just do it and I also need a piece of your clothing, but it has to be something with no buttons.

Oh, for heaven's sake Rose, are you going mad? laughed Aine. I've never heard such nonsense in my life.

Hurry up, I need these items and he wants me to go with him before sunset to break... well, what he calls the "prisoner's curse".

Aine could hardly believe what she was hearing. This sounds ridiculous Rose, but I'm willing to try anything. I know it sounds ridiculous, but you want him freed, don't you? Yes, of course, Aine replied.

Well then hurry, we have little time now.

Aine pulled a hair and placed it in an envelope. She opened up her drawer and gave Rose a knitted jumper. There that should do it.

CHAPTER 7

Time was very precious. She tucked the items under her garments trying not to any raise any suspicion as she left Aine's room.

Aine watched her from the window as she made her way across the forecourt to the outside of the castle grounds. She quietly begged to herself, please make this work. Please.

Rose made her way to the village and arrived just before sunset at John's house.

True to his word he was waiting on her. Have you got what I asked for? Yes, she replied. Let me see. She took them out and he looked over them. They must be right, he told her. Aright that's good no buttons and I don't need your envelope, thank you, just the hair. Here you take them back until I need them.

Come along, he said, it's almost sunset. We must go to `Hawthorn Hill`. With a lantern each they set of. A foggy dew was descending on the ground as they started walking.

Hawthorn Hill was a place of great mystery. No one really knew much about it although some believed that little fairy people lived there in the large Hawthorn tree that stood on the top of Hill.

As they began walking Rose thought to herself, I'll start a conversation with John, maybe he'll open up and tell me more about himself. So, em John, have you always lived in the village? Turning around and looking crossly at her, he answered. Are you going to start asking questions again like earlier? Oh goodness no. Rose quickly answered. It's just well I thought I'll be polite and mannerly seeing we are alone, and you know I am kind of curious as to what it's all about. What's what all about? Hawthorn Hill, she said. Well, if you must know, I've always been a villager. I like to keep to myself but of course I can't with this so-called special thing that I possess. Yes, about that John, Is it true that your 'a seventh son of a seventh son'. It is, he answered. So, is it true that you perform magic? Taking a deep, he stopped in the middle of the road. Look I personally don't like answering your questions because I'm sworn to secrecy. You see, it's very simple. It's called a gift. I come from a large family of boys. And it just so happened to be that I was the seventh son, the one the gift was for. It was fine in the beginning because no one bothered me. But since my father's death and because I'm next in line its now my turn to use it. So, if it bothers you that much, why don't you just refuse, Rose told him. I can't just refuse because it will bring bad luck back to me. Oh, I see, she said. That's not good then. Well, I think you should be proud of yourself for helping others. A gift is a special thing, I'm sure you'll be rewarded someday. I don't want rewards; I'd prefer to be left alone. Anyway, that's enough talking now we're almost there.

John gently opened the gate that led to the top of the hill.

Looking at Rose he explained. Now you must follow me quietly until we reach the top of the hill, and don't speak either, he told her in a low voice. Yes, she whispered back.

Off he went with Rose two steps behind him.

The climb wasn't far and arriving there he held up his hand at Rose to stop.

He stood listening and looking all around.

Alright he whispered, to Rose, they're ready. She was just about to ask who? when he said I told you not to speak, didn't I. They don't know you. You'll frighten them away.

Feeling afraid, Rose was not sure about this. Who's here? she wondered.

She followed him over to the largest hawthorn tree she'd ever seen. It was huge and ladened with beautiful white flowers. He led her underneath the blossoms.

Taking a deep breath, he whispered, give me your items and go over there and sit down opposite me. She nodded and done what he asked.

He placed the jumper Aine had given her and the lock of hair on the ground, directly between them.

Sitting down he closed his eyes.

Rose sat down placing her lantern beside her and waited... looking around not knowing who or what would appear. Ten minutes had passed.

Just then in total silence, a beautiful warm breeze started to blow around them.

It blew so softly on her face, making her smile. There was a sound like little voice's whispering in her ear making her giggle quietly.

Her hair started to sway around in the gentle breeze. Toing and froing, it felt like little hands were catching it and tossing it around.

She was feeling immense joy and happiness. Totally at ease now. Slowly a light appeared where Aine's jumper was folded on the ground in front of her.

Rose gasped at the sight but wouldn't dare say anything. Looking around she could hear music coming from behind her but could not see anything. It sounded like it was coming from the mountains far away.

Then John started to chant Alba, Alba, Mala, mala.. Come and visit us my friends. Just for a little while my friends. A chara tar isteach, meaning, friends enter in.

This continued for some time. Rose feeling a little more at ease now, could sense that something special was taking place. She had never witnessed anything like it before and was truly enjoying it. She felt a great inner peace. She knew that something good would come of this. Her hair was still being tossed around. She herself was now swaying with the breeze.

Then suddenly the items were gone, vanished before Rose's very eyes. She could barely believe it. She started looking around wondering if they'd blown away. They were nowhere to be seen.

That's so strange she thought. Of course, now I know. John told me they like gifts and this was a gift to them, so they took it. Wow this is amazing.

John's chanting started to get quieter and quieter. Alba, Alba, mala, mala.... he was now whispering.

The light was now dimming too... then disappeared. The warm breeze lessened. Rose sat there motionless.

John still had his eye's closed and had now stopped chanting. A few minutes passed and Rose thought to herself, what will I do? I hate to disturb the silence, she thought.

John, she whispered. Are you finished? Opening one eye, he said. Are you still here?

Well yes, she answered in a puzzled voice. Are you finished? Will I leave now? Yes, you may. That was fast, she said as she got up to her feet.

We have been here for two hours, he told her. Really, Rose said in a shocked voice. It was wonderful. Rose thanked him most sincerely. Thank you very much and I'm sorry for being cross with you earlier. I do hope it work's now and Fergus will be freed.

Work? Work? What do you mean work? Of course, it will work, he said as he raised his voice at her. Do you not believe in it?

Oh no I do, I'm so sorry I didn't mean it to sound like that. Please forgive me. I do believe you, really, I do.

Well, you better believe it, or it won't work.

I do, I promise and thank you. I really did enjoy this, whatever it was, it was beautiful. I'm very grateful for the experience.

As she started to walk away, John called. Wait. Rose turned quickly. Are you talking to me? she answered. Yes.... wait......there's someone else. What? Rose asked. There's another person, he said. What? Another person? She sat down slowly. John, I don't understand. What are you talking about, another person? John opened his eyes and staring blankly at her he whispered. Your brother needs you. WHAT? HOW? How do you know this? He spoke to me as you were leaving. He wants you to rescue him. His name is.... wait... it's coming to me.... Its Darragh. Rose jumped to her feet putting her hands to her face. Oh my God John how could you possibly know this. This can happen, he told her. Go on, Rose asked. Well, your brother must have been banished years ago on Hawthorn Hill.... Am I right? Yes, Rose answered, you are. But why now? Because he can channel through me if he wants, he explained. Not to give too much away...you understand this is not uncommon. Other family members that may be in distress will send messages through, and it can only happen in the very place they were banished from, which was here on Hawthorn Hill, and this is what he has done. Oh, my this is awful John. Look, he explained. Leave this for now. He's not in any danger. You asked me here to help your sister so that's what I've done. One thing at a time and don't over complicate matters. Yes, Your right. First, I must help Aine and Fergus and only then can I turn my attention to Darragh.

Go now, he told her, I must stay here all night, and remember, you must not tell anyone of this encounter.

I won't she promised and quietly left.

CHAPTER 8

Agatha had persuaded Alan not to confront Aine. She was feeling bad for Aine too. She hoped that Alan had given up on looking for Fergus, but he certainly hadn't changed his mind.

She is after all feeling very low and disappointed in herself about letting you down in this way, she told him.

This of course was not true. Aine didn't care about the Mullagh Dynasty. It meant nothing to her if she couldn't be with Fergus.

Margaret knew also that Fergus would be put to death the following morning and encouraged her father not to wait any longer as she put it "get your own back on Conall". His fate had been sealed on the day of his capture and nothing was going to change that.

Rose had made her way quietly back to the castle. On her way back she decided not to tell anyone about hearing from Darragh. Aine had enough to worry about, and she knew also that this news would deeply upset her mother. Agatha adored her only son Darragh. Over the years she secretly visited Darragh and promise him one day he'd be free again with her help. It was now 11.30. She wondered if Aine would be still awake. I'll just leave her alone and tell her in the morning. Rose was exhausted, and just needed to get a good night's sleep after the strange evening she had.

Just as she lay down in her bed a quiet knock came to the door. Rose it's Aine, let me in, quickly. Rose jumped out of bed and grabbing her night coat let Aine in.

She'd been crying. She sat down on the side of the bed. Margaret came to me after you left and told me Fergus will die tomorrow.

Rose was so angry at Margaret. Look, Aine she explained, you know I was with old man John. Yes, Aine said, listening attentively.

Well, it was very strange, but it was also very unusual, I never experienced anything quite like it before.

Catching Aine by the shoulders, she said you must believe, I must believe...we must believe together if it's going to work.

Aine was feeling very weary and with whatever little hope she had left in her heart she answered, yes Rose I believe then. I believe whatever John has done will work. Letting out a big sigh of relief, Good, said Rose. Now go to bed, I'm exhausted, and we need our sleep to get up early tomorrow. Aine agreed and went back to her room.

Lying in her bed, with tear's welling up in her eyes, Aine gazed at the starry night sky. She thought back on when she and Fergus first met.

The wonderful summer days they spent at the "water's edge". Feeling the warm summer sun on their face, they'd laugh, hold hands and talk about being together forever one day.

This day was now a far distanced memory. The night seemed to last forever. She closed her eyes tightly, praying that a miracle would happen before it would be too late.

Still awake, dawn was now breaking. She hadn't slept at all. A voice whispered at the door. Can I come in. It was Rose.

Come in. Quietly walking in Aine said to her. You're up early Rose. I just couldn't sleep at all. Oh well that makes two of us, I couldn't sleep either, Rose sighed.

They hadn't much to say to each other. Still Rose had a good feeling from the night before.

It was a truly unique experience last night Aine, Rose told her. Thank you Rose for all your doing to help me. I honestly don't know how I would have coped on my own with no one on my side. Right, Rose said, get up now and get dressed. Feeling hungry, Rose persuaded Aine to come down for breakfast.

Feeling helpless, she agreed. Her guard didn't have to accompany her when she was with Rose.

Entering the Kitchen, Imelda met her. Good morning my Lady, she said quietly to Aine. Aine whispered back, it's not a good morning, Imelda.

I know my dear I heard what was going on. Now girl's she said, sit down here and I'll bring your breakfast over. Not for me, Aine answered.

Oh, do eat something dear, you're so pale and it'll keep your strength up. No please Imelda, I don't want anything. Just bring me a glass of water.

Alright then, and you Rose. Yes, Imelda I'll have my breakfast, I'm starving.

They sat down at the end of the long wooden table.

Shortly after that Alan and Agatha came in together and not long after that Margaret. This was the first time Alan had seen Aine since the night of the Knightly Sports.

Everyone had to stand to attention as he entered the kitchen.

This was known as a "Tuback" greeting from an old ancient tradition in the "Mullagh Dynasty.

When a young boy from a Dynasty came of age, he would be knighted at a special ceremony and from then on must always be greeted in" Tuback" style.

Morning Chieftain, they said loudly as they bowed before him. Aine didn't speak. They sat down on their throne-like seats opposite Aine and Rose with a courtyard view to his left. Still angry at Aine, her father did not look at her.

Margaret was taking a side glance at Aine wondering what she was thinking but not really caring anyway.

The servant laid a feast before him. There wasn't a sound, nothing only the noise of him eating.

Aine whispered to Rose, I can't stay here. I can't look at them. They make me sick. I'm going to my room.

She got up and walking passed her father, he caught her wrist saying. You 'll wait here until we're finished eating. She quietly walked back and sat down beside Rose.

Agatha was trying to make small talk. It's a nice morning.

Oh yes mother, Margaret said gleefully. Looking over at Aine she added, we should go for a nice walk later. Rose was annoyed at Margaret for showing such joy when she knew fine well that Aine was hurting deeply inside.

Breakfast was now over. Imelda and her maids were clearing the table when all of a sudden one of the guardsmen came rushing down the great hall and into the kitchen.

Everyone turned to him. Breathless and barely able to speak he spluttered. Sir, sir. He's gone. Alan and Aine both jumped to their feet at the same time. WWHHAATTTT? Alan shouted; his roar echoed through the kitchen.

What? Who? Aine called.

The boy sir...the boy...

Aine jumped out of her seat. Looking at Rose and around the other's she asked. Do you mean Fergus?

The guard nodded his head only looking at Alan.

Alan could not believe what he was hearing. He shoved back his seat, grinding it on the floor. Rushing over to the window there was scene of chaos unfolding outside.

Guard's scurrying in and out of the cell where Fergus had been held.

Alan thumped his fist on the windowsill. How did this happen? How did this happen? he roared... someone will pay. Agatha hurried over to him followed by Margaret to see what was happening. Alan stormed out and Agatha behind him.

Aine and Rose hugged each other. Yes Rose, it actually worked, cheered Aine. I can't believe it Rose, you told me it would work. Margaret turned around. What worked? What? tell me.

We're telling you nothing, Aine told her as she run out of the kitchen. Rose said nothing, she gave Margaret a smug smile and followed Aine out.

As they ran down the hallway, they met a guard. Well, Aine asked, did Fergus escape? Yes, he did I'm afraid. I don't know how he done it, but he's gone.

Her relief at hearing this was one of complete joy. She started jumping up and down. Rose, meet me in the garden at the rear of the castle, said Aine. Rose nodded slowly.

Rose was afraid. This was truly great news. She too was shocked to learn that the spell did work.

Although the news was great, she knew that her father would be in an uncontrollable rage and feared even more now for Aine. She was too excited to see the possible danger that might unfold.

Alan summed his clansmen to his chamber known as "The Chamber of Ruckin", darkened walls and dimly lit they ushered in one-by-one bowing as they entered, HOW CAN THIS HAVE HAPPENED? Is it true he's gone? he roared. HOW? HOW? The clansmen were terrified. They'd never seen him so angry.

I'm sorry, but yes Chieftain I'm afraid so, one nervously said. Loudly and banging his fist on the table he declared. You will pay for this nodding his head, frothing as he spoke, pointing his finger ahead. Go and search the land as far as the eye can see or your entrance into the "Black Park" will be one of misery, suffering and death. His Clansmen stood in silence, for Fergus has escaped the "Black park" for now but their fate might not.

Now at this time the courtyards all around were being searched but came up fruitless.

Alan was in his quarters, when Agatha came in. Are you ok? she asked in a soft worried voice. Turning towards her he explained, Agatha my dear and loyal wife, my days are now numbered, he angrily said. This news will have reached Chieftain Conall and he will have my head.

Agatha couldn't but show her fear. But he didn't die, he's still alive, surely that's good?? yes??? How do you know women where he is, he shouted?

This has brought disgrace and agony to my kingdom, this awful alliance between these two ungrateful children. They should be the ones to suffer.

They should be banished I tell you banished... Agatha sat quietly in the hope that Alan's anger would subside, but with tears of anger in his eyes he declared I will not stand for this. I will not be the one to be fearful of that wretched Chieftain. Under my sworn oath to my ancestors, the people I rule will not be let down. Therefore, you must bring Aine to me and she must obey once and for all. Agatha's face went ashen white, clutching her chest slowly she quietly left the room knowing fine well that when Alan had something on his mind family or no family, he would keep his word.

CHAPTER 9

The day was wearing on when a guard noticed something strange at the corner of his eye on the outer rim of the castle gates, It was a soiled outer garment.

Cautiously he went to pick it up. As he approached it, he came across an open hole in the ground it was slightly covered with undergrowth and bits of twigs.

He instantly knew what this was and shouted to alert the others. OVER HERE! OVER HERE!

It wasn't long until he was surrounded, and they immediately began to unearth the scene. The hole was an open drain that came from the sewers on the inside of the castle wall, a rope had been used to descend through the sewer to get to the outside, and the garment fitted the description Fergus had been wearing.

Dalton went to inform Alan. I tell you now Dalton, he demanded. Go and get Aine for me. I need to know exactly what was going on with her and that boy. She needs to understand the importance of her poor judgment towards me. She must be punished. Now go and find her. Yes, indeed Chieftain, I will.

Rose and Aine where in the garden. Alright Rose said in a firm voice. I've been thinking, you need to leave now, run away.

Naively, Aine questioned. But why Rose? Do you think that would be best? Yes, Rose replied.

Listen Aine. Fergus might have gotten away but your still here. What do you mean by that? I mean that it was you and Fergus that started this and now he's gone you're the next one father might.... well... you know. What Rose? you actually think father would... KILL me? she slowly said.

Rose gave her a sickening look. Aine I'm so sorry but yes, I do think he is capable of that. Aine clasped her mouth with her hand.

Well, that's that then, I need to get out of here right now. But where? Where could I possibly go? I have a good friend Sarah that lives' outside the village, explained Rose. She won't mind you staying with her for a while. I'll take you to her. But what about Fergus, Rose, I want to be with him.

Listen, let's get you away from here first, then and only then can we see what happens going forward. But discreetly, Aine, they will be watching your every move so don't alert anyone. Keep out of everyone's view for now.

Yes, Rose I understand. I'll get my thing's ready. Aine hurried away.

Agatha joined Rose. She sat down on the bench beside her. Mother you look so sad. I know this must be very difficult for you, but

it's very difficult for Aine too. Agatha was quiet. Tears rolled down her face. Oh mother, Rose said as she comforted her.

I'm so sorry for you too, deeply sorry.

Rose, my dear child, I'm in despair for Aine. Your father's fury is like no other and I fear him greatly, she sobbed. Perhaps I should have never told him.

Listen to me Rose, I want you to take Aine away from here...as soon as you can...today?

Rose was stunned to hear this. Mother, we have already made this plan, myself and Aine. She turned to look at Rose. Really? You have?

Yes, Rose answered. I fear for her life too. With a sincere look on her face, Agatha turned to Rose and catching her two hands, she said. Rose....He will kill her. I'm telling you now, get her away from this place today.

I still mourn my beloved son Darragh. You see, I've been to see Darragh. I just had to see him. I worry deeply about him and he's coming home soon. Rose, I am not, do you hear me, I am not going to mourn another child. Mother that is great to hear. How is Darragh. He's fine, she reassured her, much better than I expected. Anyway, that's for another day, now go quickly and don't tell Margaret.

Rose was delighted to hear the news her mother told her about visiting Darragh. She was so relieved to know that he was in good health. Yes mother. I will. Rose ran off to find Aine.

Margaret never suspected a thing. She stayed with her beloved father until he was feeling calmer and reassuring him that she would help him to "get the problem dealt with". She meant Aine was the problem and she needed to be dealt with.

It was now late afternoon.

Rose and Aine were making final arrangements. So, you know what you must do? I've already sent Jacob (the gateman) with the telegram for Sarah. She will be waiting for you outside the village. Yes Rose. I understand. I've got what I need for now, Aine told her.

Alright... Rose went on to explain, do you know where Rhododendron Lane is?

Oh my, Rose, she sighed, of course I know. That's beside the "water's edge" where I would meet Fergus.

Great, you know it then. I will bring you to the village and you wait at Rhododendron Lane for Sarah. She will collect you there. I cannot wait with you for fear of alerting Margaret or father. What about Mother? Aine asked her.

Rose explained, mother is very worried about you too. She confided in me earlier after you left the garden and believes you are in danger and will help you in any way.

We must not let anyone else know of this though. We need to protect mother. If father finds out, she too will suffer.

Aine was glad to hear of her mother's approval. This had weighed heavily on her mind. Running away from her was not a nice thing to do.

She loved her mother dearly. We will have to wait till later perhaps when it's getting a little darker.

Aine agreed, Rose went off to find her mother, to let her know their plan.

It was nearing 8 o'clock and night was falling. Rose had arranged with her mother to stay with her father and Margaret all evening.

Agatha hugged and kissed Aine. My dear child, she cried, I'm sorry you must do this awful act. I pray one day you will return to me and that you'll be happy to do so. Mother, Aine told her, I don't want you to be sad. If I have to go for now, then that's the best thing for me to do. I promise, I will come back. I do love you dear mother and father, but I must do this.

I need to go; Rose will be waiting for me downstairs. Rose had organised with Jacob, to escort them to the village.

Yes, Agatha agreed. Go and I'll come and see you soon. She went to the study where Alan and Margaret were.

It never entered their minds that Aine was going to leave. Dalton not knowing either, thought to himself he had plenty of time to capture Aine.

Aine quietly rushed downstairs and outside to the back of the castle. Rose and Jacob where waiting.

You have my suitcase, Rose? Yes, now jump into the carriage. In she got, quietly and slowly they rode off. Aine had a lump in her throat.

Looking back at the castle she felt lonely. I can't believe it's come to this, she thought. And just because I love another.

Poor mother, I will come back to see you, she whispered to herself.

The village was quiet. Over there Jacob, Rose pointed. Go over there. Cautiously they rode towards Rhododendron Lane. He pulled on the horse's reins.

Wow, wow boy. There was no time for goodbyes. Rose jumped out followed by Aine. Here take your suitcase, wait and Sarah will be here soon.

She gave her a quick hug and explained that she would see her very soon. Please bring mother too, said Aine. Off course, I must leave.

Yes, go, and waving goodbye Rose left.

Aine stood quietly. It was cold and the night was quite dark now. Suddenly, there he was... waiting. Fergus came out from Rhododendron Lane.

OH my goodness, she gleefully cheered. Fergus ran to hug her. I can't believe it, I mean, how? How did you know I'd be here? Rose told me. Rose? she said with shock... How... how was that possible?

I've missed you so much Fergus. Hugging one another, he promised to not lose her again. Fergus took the letter out of his pocket.

You wrote this before I was captured, remember? Rose had Jacob give it to me, before I escaped. How did you escape?

I was so happy when I heard this, Aine told him.

I didn't think I'd ever be able to escape. It was around sunset, when I seen a rope in the corner of the cell. It wasn't there before. I would have seen it because I'd been looking for ways to escape. It just kind of miraculously appeared as if someone had put it there. Aine nodding her head, listening, knew that this was the magic that John performed on Hawthorn Hill. I escaped through the sewer; it wasn't difficult at all.

Anyway, I'm here now and I'm not going to leave you again. Were you here all day waiting for me? Aine asked.

Yes, well kind off. When I escaped, the workhouse took me in, and I got washed. They gave me clean clothes. I knew the wait wouldn't be too long, as Jacob explained to me, you'd be here shortly after dark. I'll go with you to Sarah's house and then I'm taking you to Hendro.

You'll be safe there with me. What about your family asked Aine, will I be accepted there? Oh yes you will, they know already.

We shall stay here a few weeks until my family make final arrangements. Then we will leave... together.

CHAPTER 10

Three weeks had passed, and winter had begun.

Alan knew by now that Aine had run away. He wasn't too bothered by that. He was more thinking of himself. He feared a battle could still be imminent if Chieftain Conall decided to act against him for holding Fergus captive.

Over the weeks, Rose and her mother would secretly visit Aine as often as they could. So happy to be with them again.

Aine found it very difficult when they had to part. They would reminisce on day's passed and what could have been if it hadn't been for her father's anger and traditions.

The times they'd spent together was now coming to an end. An easterly winter wind blew on the morning of their departure.

Fergus had gotten word that arrangement's had been made for himself and Aine to come and live in Hendro.

Agatha was deeply torn by this situation. She knew that for Aine to be truly happy she would have to let her go for good.

To not see her face again was a heart-breaking thought. This was the ultimate sacrifice and Hendro was far away.

She also feared Alan greatly. If he was ever to find out that Agatha was somewhat involved with helping Aine, she would certainly not be forgiven and feared for her life.

You have me mother, Rose would encouragingly tell her.

Oh, dear Rose, I know and I'm deeply grateful for that, but I can't bear to think of losing you Aine. You're not losing me mother, Aine explained.

I can make visit's back to the village. This is what I want more than anything right now and although it seems selfish, I promise I will come back when I can.

Hugging Aine tightly with tears in her eyes, her mother told her, I love you dearly. Turning to Fergus, and catching his hand she asked him, please take care of my child. He responded quietly telling her, not to worry and that he would keep her safe.

Aine hugged her mother. I love you too mother and please tell Margaret I'm sorry and I hope she forgives me. Nodding, her mother reassured her that she would.

Sarah had arranged for her brother Cormac to take them part of the journey.

Taking them the whole journey to the province of Hendro was going to be too long. Chieftain Conall's family had arranged to meet them at a place called "Mac Croary's height". This was a mountainous border crossing into Hendro. Once they crossed the border, they would be safe and free from Alan's clansmen.

Thanking Sarah for her goodness for providing them with a safe house, they finally set of at noon. Aine was filled with emotion, excitement and sadness.

Wrapped up in warm clothing they rode off. She watched Rose and her mother wipe the tears from their face. She blew them a kiss and called, thank you and I love you.

Disappearing out of sight, Fergus put his arm around Aine, whispering no one can separate us anymore. You will be happy in Hendro.

My family will welcome you with great affection. This assurance was just what Aine needed to hear.

They had been travelling for about two hours now and Mac Croary's Height was insight. Fergus and Aine were filled with excitement now.

They only had a few minutes to go and they would be safely cross the border. Aine could hardly believe that after all she'd been through, finally, she was getting away from the clutches of her father.

No more being locked in her room. No more secret meetings with Fergus. For the first time in her life, she felt free.

Cormac pulled on the horse to stop. There's no one here, he said. Jumping onto the ground Fergus thought that was strange.

Are they not here? asked Aine. Don't worry, they'll be here, fergus reassured her.

They took the suitcase's off. I can wait with you, Cormac explained. No, no there's no need for that. I know my family will have sent someone. Unknown to them, the horsemen that were to meet them got held up after the horse bolted the trap.

They won't be long. You get back Cormac before dark, Fergus told him. Aine wasn't sure. Are you sure Fergus? she worryingly asked him.

What if something happened and they don't come. Fergus laughed, don't be worrying, they will come. Now go Cormac, we will be fine.

Cormac was happy to leave as he didn't want to get stranded out there in darkness.

Although Fergus was reassuring Aine, he was a little concerned about the situation. It was somewhat unusual that no one was there for them.

An hour had passed and still no one had arrived. Fergus, I'm not happy about this, it's very cold perhaps we should start walking back.

No Aine, I've a better idea. I know a short cut over the mountain and we're closer to Hendro so there's no point turning back. She agreed and taking Fergus's hand of they went on a perilous journey up the mountain. They were walking for a while now and Aine's legs were getting tired.

Can we sit for a while? Alright Aine, but not too long as it'll get dark very soon.

Sitting together on a large stone, they took in the beautiful scenery. They talked about their future and how much Aine was looking forward to meeting Fergus family and visiting the Province of Hendro.

Pointing southwards, Fergus explained, thats the lights of Hendro Aine. We will be so happy there. We don't have too far to go now, she thought. Oh, good Fergus, cause I'm very cold.

On hearing that, he was concerned for Aine. Let's go then. We'll make it before dark.

As they slowly got up and started walking, it began to snow heavily. Aine had always loved the snow. Many happy days she and her sisters would have inside the castle grounds playing in it. But she wasn't too fond of it now. A worrying feeling came over her. Fergus we must walk faster. This is not good; the snow fall is much heavier up here. Yes, he agreed.

Holding hands and heads down they plunged on. It was falling much heavier now, blizzard like.

The wind was stronger too, they were breathless...Oh please, please make it stop, Fergus shouted. Aine began to cry a little. Looking at Fergus face, she could see that he was frightened. Struggling to get the words out she said, Fergusss...her teeth chattering. Are you alright?

Shaking now with the cold he answered...I think so. Desperately trying to be brave to not worry Aine. She was so frightened. The wind not letting up, could be heard howling through the valleys below.

Fergus now knew in his heart, that they should have waited, thinking to himself their probably at the border now waiting for us.

It was too late now for turning back. Trying to take bigger steps, they were getting slower, and the snow was getting deeper.

Desperately they pushed on. Their true love for one another was determined to push them on, up the cruel rugged mountain.

Ahhhh, Aine cried out, I can't Fergus, I can't walk anymore.

I just can't go any further.

Barely able to talk and feeling so isolated it was almost impossible to hear each other now with the loud wind.

The harshness of the cruel winter snow was now their biggest enemy.

Worn out and fatigued, they fell to the ground.

It was simply too tough. Their bodies weakening all the time with the raging wind.

Fergus caught Aine as she fell. I'm so sorry, he cried, I shouldn't have brought you this way.

Her voice weaker now told Fergus, it's not your fault Fergus. Please don't blame yourself. I love you...He hugged her tightly. I love you too...

They sat, held each other and listened. With a feeling of despair and anguish in their hearts.

Desperately hoping and praying it would stop or someone would find them.

They were too weak now to continue the treacherous journey, there was simply nothing more they could do. Just waiting and hoping.... the piercing cold winter wind would not let up.

The distanced lights of Hendro had now disappeared in the blizzard.

Fergus held Aine's cold hand, now a shade of blue.

Resting his head on hers, and quietly whispering he said. My darling Aine, keep strong.... help will come....

We will be rescued. The heavy snow had blowen a white blanket around where they sat almost covering them.

Aine was now silent. Time passed so slowly.

PLease, please help us, Fergus cried out.......please...save us...please.... nothing only the sound of the wind.

Squeezing Aine's hand he knew it was too late for help......
Aine, he cried out. Please Aine...don't leave me, please, her
little cold hand didn't squeeze back.

He raised her up... her head fell back...Aine was gone.
Noooooo....Fergus cried out. Tears streaming from his eye's.

No more would he see her beautiful brown eyes.

The dreams they shared had disappeared in the winter
wind.

Fergus heart that had been so filled with love was now
empty and broken.

Her lifeless body lay on his chest.......his only movement
were the tears falling from his face and resting on her pale
forehead.

......and quietness......Knowing Aine was gone.... he sobbed
and kissed her cold face and whispered...Ta mo chroi duitse
amhain my beautiful lady in red.

Closing his eyes for the last time he took his last breath,
and he too was gone.

> They lived,
> and loved,
> and laughed,
> and left.

Written by Frances Maguire.

Lightning Source UK Ltd.
Milton Keynes UK
UKHW040626100222
398405UK00015B/53